YOU CHOOSE

THE EMPEROR'S NEW CLOTHES

AN INTERACTIVE FAIRY TALE ADVENTURE

You Choose Books are published by Capstone Press, an imprint of Capstone.
1710 Roe Crest Drive
North Mankato, Minnesota 56003
www.capstonepub.com

Library of Congress Cataloging-in-Publication data is available on the Library of
Congress website.
ISBN 978-1-5435-9011-1 (library binding)
ISBN 978-1-4966-5811-1 (paperback)
ISBN 978-1-5435-9015-9 (eBook PDF)

Summary: Using a choose-your-own-format, readers navigate their way through
three twisted versions of the classic fairy tale "The Emperor's New Clothes."

Editorial Credits
Editor: Michelle Parkin; Designer: Brann Garvey; Media Researcher: Eric Gohl;
Production Specialist: Kathy McColley

Printed and bound in the USA.
PA100

TABLE OF CONTENTS

ABOUT YOUR ADVENTURE

Dealing with someone who's vain and selfish can be hard, especially when they have power over you. Over time, you get used to it. But when two strangers come to town, the world as you know it is changed forever.

In this fairy tale, you control your fate. Put on your finest clothes and choose what happens next.

Chapter One sets the scene. Then you choose which path to read. Follow the directions at the bottom of the page as you read the stories. The decisions you make will change your outcome. After you finish one path, go back and read the others for new perspectives and more adventures.

CHAPTER 1

ALL ABOUT STYLE

YOU are a member of a powerful group of people. You call the leader the Emperor. The Emperor is a nice enough person, but also someone who cares a lot about appearances and having a good time. The Emperor doesn't pay much attention to boring things like rules and responsibilities.

One thing the Emperor *does* like is praise. People showing up to ooh and ahh over the newest and greatest accessories is the Emperor's favorite pastime. And the Emperor loves parades. But mostly just to show off fancy clothes and other fancy things.

You've known the Emperor for a long time. You consider yourself to be a close friend. Well, as close a friend as the Emperor can have, anyway.

While the Emperor can get on your nerves, you enjoy being so important. There are a lot of perks to being in the Emperor's inner circle. You get the best tables at restaurants. You pose for photos. People look up to you. And you have to admit, those parades *are* pretty fun.

One day, two people you've never seen before approach the Emperor. They brag about all the famous people they know and what they've done for them. They say they can make the Emperor's status soar.

What they say sounds amazing. Almost too amazing. The Emperor is hanging on their every word, but you aren't so sure. You don't trust these newcomers.

To be a sheriff in the Old West, turn to page 11.

To be an advisor on the moon, turn to Page 41.

To be the bestie of a fancy foodie, turn to page 73.

CHAPTER 2

BEST DRESSED IN THE WEST

Howdy, partner! This here town is Rattlesnake Hill, and you are the sheriff. You love it. The town has a bank, saloons, and even a theater. The sky over the frontier is vast and blue. At sunset, the hills glow a beautiful rose color. Some say there's gold in those hills, and lots of city slickers have gone after it. But mostly, folks work hard and make an honest living.

There is the occasional criminal or two. Now and again you get some rascally scoundrels in town. Around here, though, people don't take kindly to mischief-makers. Trouble is usually easy to see coming, like a storm moving in across the dusty plain.

So what do you make of these two strangers who come to town? They say they can make the finest clothing this side of the Mississippi. Well, that sure got the mayor's attention. But something about them doesn't sit right with you.

Everybody knows Mayor Augustus is a vain man. He wears silk shirts and Italian leather britches. He even has a big ten-gallon hat with ostrich feathers. Heck, who has even seen an ostrich out here? His gun belt is encrusted with rubies and emeralds. He dresses so fancy that some of the locals have a secret nickname for him. They call him the Emperor. You have to admit—it kind of fits.

"These clothes aren't just the most handsome in the land," one of the strangers says. "They also have a magical quality to them."

"Do tell," says Mayor Augustus. He wiggles his fingers excitedly.

The stranger smiles. He lowers his voice. "Anyone who is unworthy of their position cannot see them."

"You will know who is not doing a good job," adds the second stranger. "You will know who is not loyal to you!"

The mayor's face lights up. He is actually bouncing in his chair like a toddler.

"We shall use the money from the bridge fund," he says.

You frown. The bridge fund is supposed to fix the bridge on the main road that crosses the creek. It has been falling apart for months.

Turn the page.

Without that bridge, people have to ride miles downstream in order to cross the water. There is no other way to go to the next town.

"If we use that money, the bridge will not be repaired," you remind the mayor. But he has made up his mind, and he pays the men.

Two days later, you sit in the courthouse with Harlan, the deputy. The mayor comes in.

"Someone go check on my new clothes," the mayor says. "I must know how they are coming along."

"Don't you want to see for yourself, sir?" Harlan asks.

"I don't want to appear too eager," the mayor answers.

To check on the mayor's clothes, go to page 15.

To send Harlan to check on the clothes, turn to page 18.

You walk down the dusty street to the hotel where the strangers are staying. The hotel clerk tells you which room they are in, and you head upstairs. As you walk down the hallway, the floorboards squeak under your feet. Suddenly the you hear a spinning wheel start up behind a door.

You knock.

"Just a moment," one of the men says. "We're very busy. We are working so hard, we can barely stop to answer the door!"

You hear rustling, and finally the door opens. One of the men stands before you. "Come in," he says. "My name is Clyde, by the way."

"Good afternoon, Clyde," you say, tipping your hat. "I'm the sheriff. Mayor Augustus has sent me to check on your progress."

Turn the page.

"Of course, of course," Clyde says, gesturing to his partner. "Butch, show the sheriff the mayor's clothes."

You look to the weaving loom where Butch is sitting. He lifts his hand at the end of the machine, as if he's showing you something. But you don't see anything!

"What is the meaning of this?" you ask.

"What do you mean, sir?" says Butch. "Do you not approve of the quality? I assure you, these are the finest materials you will ever see."

16   You remember what the men said about the clothes. If someone cannot see them, that means the person is not worthy of his position. You are not sure if you believe them or not. But you are quite sure the mayor does.

To confront the men, turn to page 20.
To pretend you can see the clothes, turn to page 22.

"Why don't you go, Harlan?" you say. "It's time for me to patrol the town."

You put on your hat and head out into the hot afternoon. You walk around Rattlesnake Hill's small downtown, keeping your eyes peeled for trouble. You are a good sheriff. People feel safe with you wearing that tin star.

You stop at the Tumbleweed Café for a bite to eat. While you are enjoying your bacon and grits, you overhear two men talking at a table nearby.

"A fool and his money are soon parted," one of them says.

The other laughs. "And we got us a right fool this time."

You recognize the men. They arrived in town at the same time as the tailors. Could they be talking about the mayor's new clothes?

After you're finished with your meal, you walk over to the Rattlesnake Hotel. You see a black and gold carriage parked along the side. It belongs to the two tailors. You peek in the window. Two trunks are stowed in the back. One is partly open. You see what looks like the fine silk that the mayor gave the tailors to make his clothes. You better talk to Harlan.

Back at the office, you take Harlan aside. "How do the new clothes look?"

"Why do you ask?" he says nervously. "They look great. They are very fancy."

You keep pressing, but he doesn't say anything different. He also never tells you what the clothes look like.

To go check the clothes for yourself, turn to page 25.

To wait for the tailors to bring the clothes, turn to page 27.

"There is nothing on that loom!" you say. "Who do you think you are fooling?"

"With all due respect, sheriff, I must disagree," says Butch. "I feel we have truly outdone ourselves. This is our best work yet!"

"Perhaps your best thievery," you say. "But you will not get away with it!"

"Oh, my," Clyde says, shaking his head sadly. "Are you saying you cannot see the clothing here on the loom? Oh, dear, this is not good news for you."

"On behalf of Mayor Augustus, I demand you return all funds and materials," you say.

Butch picks up a six-shooter on the table next to the loom. "You sure you want to do that, partner? Maybe you are accusing us of forgery to cover your tracks."

"You have a choice to make here, sheriff,"
Clyde adds, lowering Butch's gun. "You could tell
the mayor that his new clothes are not real. If he
doesn't believe you, you lose your job. Your other
choice? Tell him the clothes are the finest in
the land."

"I know which one I'd choose," Butch says.

Of course, there is a third choice.

To tell the mayor he's being cheated, turn to page 29.

To say the clothes look great, turn to page 31.

To arrest the men, turn to page 33.

"Um," you stammer. "They're lovely!"

"Thank you," Butch says. "What do you think of the stitching here?"

"Oh," you say, "I was just noticing how nice that stitch is. The mayor will be pleased."

When you get back to the courthouse, the mayor is on you immediately. "Well?" he asks. "How do my new clothes look?"

"I couldn't believe my eyes," you say truthfully.

"Oh, boy!" The mayor says, jumping up and down. "We must have a parade to celebrate."

A few days later, Clyde and Butch show up at the courthouse with a wooden crate. You watch the mayor carefully as he opens the box. He stares inside. Then he lets out a low whistle.

"Wow!" he says. "These are beautiful."

"Try them on," Clyde insists. He pulls out an invisible article of clothing and holds it out. You still don't see a thing. But the mayor takes the invisible clothes into his office. He comes out a few minutes later—wearing only his underwear.

"How do I look?" he says.

"Uh . . . well, I've never seen anything like it," you say.

The day of the parade, the mayor dresses in his new clothes and gets in his open-air carriage. Main Street is crowded with families as the parade marches down the town. The mayor rides by, waving to everyone with a big smile on his face. His undershirt ripples in the breeze.

"Hey!" a man calls from the street. "The mayor's not wearing any clothes!"

The parade screeches to a halt. The mayor points to the man.

"Arrest him!" the mayor yells to you.

24   You do as you are told. You grab the man and take him to the small cell at the courthouse. The mayor wants him to spend years behind bars.

All the man did was tell the truth. You will never forget the shameful day you threw an innocent man in jail.

THE END
To follow another path, turn to page 9.

You go to the strangers' hotel room and knock on the door. "It's the sheriff!" you say. "Let me in!"

"We're busy now," one of them says from inside. "Come back later."

"I am here now. I demand to see the mayor's new clothes." You keep knocking.

A moment later, the door opens. One of the strangers stands before you, smiling. "I'm sorry to keep you waiting," he apologizes. "The deputy already came by. You must be really excited to see what we've done."

The stranger introduces himself as Clyde. His partner is named Butch. Across the room, Butch sits working at a loom. But the loom itself is empty. There is no cloth on it. There is no thread. As you watch, though, Butch lifts his hand away from his lap as if pulling a thread through a piece of fabric. Is this a joke?

"What do you think?" he asks you, pretending to hold up a shirt.

"I think I'd like to know what you've done with the money the mayor gave you," you say.

"You cannot see the clothes, sir?" Clyde asks. "That means you are unworthy of your position. Perhaps this town needs a new sheriff."

"You can't fool me," you say, drawing your gun. "I saw the silk in your carriage. Give me the money back—now!"

"Wait!" Butch says. He and his partner exchange glances. "How would you like to join us? I know sheriffs don't make much money. Why not come with us? We could use a gunman."

"And we pay well," Clyde adds.

To join the men, turn to page 35.

To arrest them, turn to page 38.

26

You decide to wait. Two days later, the men arrive at the courthouse with a box. They set it down in the mayor's office and open it. Inside, there is nothing. The box is empty.

"Aren't they beautiful?" the tailor named Clyde says.

"Just like I told you the other day," Harlan says. "Those are some amazing clothes."

The mayor looks confused.

"Is something wrong?" Clyde asks.

"Yes," the mayor says. "There *is* something wrong." The mayor is not so crazy after all. But then he says, "There's not enough! I wish I had ordered more! They are wonderful!"

The mayor goes to his office to try on the clothes. When he comes out, he is wearing nothing but his underwear.

That week the mayor has a grand parade. He rides in an open-air carriage to show off his new outfit. A few townspeople laugh as the mayor passes by in his underwear. But Mayor Augustus doesn't seem to notice. In fact, he wears his new clothes every day after the parade.

The people start to get angry. That bridge still hasn't been repaired. They paid their taxes. They need that bridge. But the mayor spent all of their money on himself.

That is when you decide *you* will run for mayor. The election is coming up, and the mayor is very unpopular. You promise to fix the bridge. You promise that no town money can be spent on an official's personal clothing ever again. You are certain you will win.

THE END
To follow another path, turn to page 9.

"You underestimate the mayor," you tell the men. "He is not quite the fool you think he is."

You return to the courthouse and report the news to Mayor Augustus.

"The tailors are fakes," you say. "They plan to keep the silk, pocket the money, and give you nothing. They think you will believe there are really clothes."

The mayor rubs his chin, thinking. "I see," he says. But when the men arrive with the clothes, the mayor turns to Harlan first. "Deputy," he says, "what do you think of these clothes?"

"Remember," one of the tailors warns, "anyone who cannot see these clothes is disloyal to the mayor and to Rattlesnake Hill."

Turn the page.

Harlan looks to the mayor, who is eyeing the invisible clothing with obvious pleasure. "I, well, I think they are fantastic, sir," Harlan stammers. "You will look wonderful in these clothes."

"Yes," the mayor says. "I agree." He turns to you. "You're fired. Turn over your badge. Harlan, you are the sheriff now."

You start to protest, but you see that you are outnumbered. Everyone in the room is pretending to see the mayor's glorious new outfit. Maybe you should have done the same. You give up your badge and your gun. Every day after that, you see Sheriff Harlan patrolling the town of Rattlesnake Hill. You wonder if the truth really has any meaning at all.

30

THE END

To follow another path, turn to page 9.

You have to admit that the mayor is easily swayed. He will believe anything if he thinks it will make him look good. The smart choice would be to say that the mayor's clothes are real.

When the tailors deliver the goods to the courthouse a few days later, you and Harlan both fawn over the invisible items.

"Oh, wow," you say. "They sure are wonderful."

"Boy, howdy," agrees Harlan.

That week, the mayor wears his new outfit in a parade. He is carried down the street, proudly looking over the people of Rattlesnake Hill. The townspeople gawk at him in stunned silence. Finally, a small boy speaks up.

"The mayor has no clothes!" he says. The townspeople erupt in laughter.

Turn the page.

The mayor looks out, embarrassed. He knows the boy is telling the truth.

That day the mayor fires you and Harlan for not arresting the crooks. You can't blame him. You didn't do your job. You are ashamed of yourself. You decide it's high time to move on to a new town—after the bridge is fixed.

THE END

To follow another path, turn to page 9.

The men are criminals, and you are the sheriff. There is really only one thing you can rightly do—arrest them. But you decide to wait until you have backup. Butch is waving his pistol around, and you are outnumbered.

You pretend to agree to the tailors' plan. Then you return to the courthouse and tell Harlan about the invisible clothes. You and the deputy decide to wait for the men to leave the hotel this evening for dinner. That's when you will arrest them.

You and Harlan station yourselves on the porch of the courthouse and keep an eye out. Soon enough, the men emerge from the hotel. They head toward the Tumbleweed Café.

Turn the page.

"Hold it!" you call out. You have your pistols aimed at them. "Put your hands up. I aim to put you in a cell for fraud against the mayor of Rattlesnake Hill!"

Clyde and Butch freeze. For a moment, nothing happens.

"I said, hands up!" you remind them.

Suddenly, with twitchlike speed, Butch reaches for his two six-shooters. The barrels blaze, and Harlan falls to the dirt. You fire and miss. Something hits your chest. The sky seems to turn from blue to white in a flash. You drop to your knees.

They might not be good tailors, you think, *but that Butch is a heck of a good shooter.*

THE END
To follow another path, turn to page 9.

"I *am* in need of money," you admit. "More than I can earn with this job."

"Yee-haw!" Clyde exclaims, shaking your hand. "All right then, partner. All you got to do for now is play along. Make sure that crazy mayor believes in these clothes. Then we make our getaway during the parade."

When the men show up with the invisible clothing in a box, you act like they are very fine indeed. Harlan agrees, of course. He is too scared to disagree with the mayor. The mayor loves his clothes and wears them in the parade. At first, the crowd is cheering. Everyone is afraid to say that the clothes are not real. Nobody wants to be seen as unworthy. You hop in Clyde and Butch's carriage and ride away.

Turn the page.

But someone must have said something. When you glance back at the town, you can see the parade is breaking up. It's too early! There is a big ruckus. You spot a posse of men chasing you on horseback.

"They're after us!" you yell. Butch urges the horses to go faster. The creek is up ahead.

"Wait!" you say, remembering the crumbling bridge. "We can't get across that."

But it is too late. Butch races the carriage toward the bridge. At first, it seems like the bridge will hold. But then you hear a beam snap.

"Just a little farther!" Clyde says.

But you do not make it. The bridge collapses sideways, and the carriage tips. You hit the wood planks as the bridge drops into the water. Silk in dozens of colors, fine gold threads, and other fancy linens tumble into the water. Coins, paper money, and even gold bars clatter against the rocks and scatter. Clyde and Butch gather up as much as they can and run off on foot. But you have broken your leg. You lie along the bank and wait to be arrested.

THE END
To follow another path, turn to page 9.

"Sorry, boys," you say, pulling out your handcuffs. "I'm a man of the law. I'm taking you in. It's time to pay the price for your life of crime."

Butch reaches for his pistol, but you are too quick. You knock it away from his grasp. Butch and Clyde put their hands up.

You lead the men down the street to the courtroom, where you put them in jail. You explain everything to Mayor Augustus and Deputy Harlan. The mayor is pleased.

"Very good work, sheriff," he says. But then he slumps onto a bench and lets out a loud sigh.

"I'm sorry about the clothes, sir," you say. "Perhaps we can find a real tailor to make you some."

"Sheriff, you are the only one I can trust," he says to you. "I have a plan."

His plan is for *you* to sew his new clothes. For the next several weeks, you take lessons from a local seamstress and work on new clothes for the mayor. Instead of fighting crime, you spend your days in the back room of the courthouse cutting, stitching, and sewing. You are not good at it. But the mayor insists that you do the job. The clothes you make are clumsy and ugly. They have poor stitching and ragged seams. Finally you show them to the mayor.

"These are the finest in the land!" you say. "And they have a magical quality. Anyone who can't see their beauty is unworthy of their position."

You hope it will work. It seems like the kind of thing the mayor would believe.

THE END
To follow another path, turn to page 9.

CHAPTER 3

LUNAR LUNACY

It finally happened. Humans built a community on the moon. As climate change made life on Earth more and more dangerous, people were desperate to find a new place to live.

The moon nation was created as a democracy. You elected a government with a president who shared lawmaking power with a group of senators. But it wasn't long before the president wanted more and more power. He made laws against poor people, and he ignored the senate's objections. He created a secret police to enforce his policies. He made it illegal to disagree with him.

Eventually, the president declared that the senate was illegal. He dissolved it, and all the senators mysteriously disappeared. Some people said the president had them sent to a distant space station. Others think he had them killed. After the senate was gone, he changed his title from president to Emperor.

You are one of the Emperor's closest advisors. You know he is corrupt and dangerous. He is also very vain. He loves to get compliments on his hair and clothes, even if he's not on point all the time.

One day two strangers, Scarlett and Luisa, appear at the Emperor's mansion. They request a meeting. They say they are excellent tailors. They would like a job with the Emperor. Scarlett brags that she can make him the finest spacesuit ever. This spacesuit will even have magical properties.

"You are in a dangerous position," Scarlett explains to the Emperor. "Because of your power, people everywhere would love to betray you and overthrow you. But this spacesuit will help you find out who those traitors are. Anyone who has betrayal in their heart will not be able to see the suit!"

Luisa jumps in. "If anyone tells you they can't see it, you will know you can't trust them. It's the only way to keep your power."

The Emperor loves this idea. He quickly agrees to pay the tailors a huge sum of money. They take the cash and run off to do their work. **43**

Two days later, the Emperor comes to you with a request.

Turn the page.

"I want you to check on the tailors' progress," the Emperor tells you. "I'm not sure we can trust them."

"Of course," you say, and head off.

You find the tailors hard at work in a room in the Emperor's mansion. He let them stay while they produce the suit. But when you walk in, you can see that there is no material on the table. Either the suit is invisible—which means that you're a traitor—or there is no suit at all.

You've never thought of yourself as a traitor. Removing the Emperor would be very dangerous. Still, maybe it is true. Maybe deep down, you want him out of power.

"What do you think?" Scarlett asks. "Amazing, isn't it?" She runs her hand over the table, as though she is touching fabric.

You are about to answer when realize you've seen the tailors before. They are former senators! The Emperor didn't recognize them. He was so focused on his power grab that he didn't bother to learn who everyone was.

To confront the tailors, turn the page.

To pretend you see the spacesuit, turn to page 48.

"Senators, I know what you are doing," you say. "There is no spacesuit here. Do you think you can deceive the Emperor so easily?"

"What?" says Luisa. "You cannot see this suit sitting right here before your eyes? You must be a traitor to the Emperor!"

"Come on," you say. "This is lunacy. There is *nothing there*." You walk over and put your hand on the worktable. You feel nothing but table.

Luisa and Scarlett say nothing for a moment. Then Scarlett says, "We don't see anything either."

It takes you a moment to realize what Scarlett is saying. They are traitors.

"You know I could have you arrested," you say.

"You could do that," Scarlett agrees. "And we will be put in prison for treason. And everything will go on as it has been. The Emperor will continue to cause pain and death with his cruel laws. The people will become poorer while the Emperor becomes wealthier and wealthier."

"You will always worry," Luisa adds. "'Is he going to have me killed next?' 'Will I be safe?'"

47

"What do you suggest?" you ask.

"Help us get rid of him," Scarlett says.

To turn them in, turn to page 51.

To join their plot, turn to page 55.

Scarlett and Luisa look at you patiently while you decide what to say. You realize that it is too risky to admit that you can't see the suit. In the Emperor's mind, it doesn't matter if there is any proof. If he believes you are a traitor, then you are a traitor.

"It's wonderful," you say with a fake smile. "Great work. I especially like the, uh, fancy stars on the chest. The Emperor will be delighted."

"You mean the badges? Oh, good," Luisa says. "We are so glad you approve."

You report back to the Emperor. You say that the suit is coming along nicely. You tell him about the fancy badges on the chest.

"Oh, it is even better than I hoped," the Emperor says.

The next day he sends another advisor, Boris, to check on the suit. Boris comes back quickly with a report even more glowing than yours.

"The suit is a masterpiece!" Boris exclaims. "Intelligent life from all over the galaxy will be coming just to see it. They will want to meet you, of course. Only a very powerful leader could possibly have such a suit."

At this, the Emperor almost falls off of his chair from excitement. After he leaves, you grab Boris's arm.

"Did you notice the coloring on the badges?" you ask Boris.

"Of course," he says. "They were, um, gold and purple. And, uh, green?" He clears his throat. "Right?"

"They were silver," you say.

"Oh, right!" Boris says. "That's what I meant."

You breathe a sigh of relief. Boris doesn't see the suit either.

"Boris," you whisper. "It's okay."

"What's okay?" he asks.

"The spacesuit," you say. "I know you don't see it."

"I *do* see it," he says. "I swear."

"Boris," you say. "I don't see it either."

He looks at the door that leads to the **50** Emperor's inner chamber. "Okay, I cannot see the suit," Boris sighs. "What do we do now?"

"Now we have a big decision to make," you say.

To say nothing to the Emperor, turn to page 63.

To tell the Emperor, turn to page 66.

You can't risk getting involved in a plot to overthrow the Emperor. If it fails, you will be punished along with them. You know that the Emperor is corrupt. His laws have hurt people, and his secret police are dangerous. Things aren't getting any better under his rule. But you have to watch out for the people you love.

"Sure," you lie to Scarlett and Luisa. "I'm on your side." You need to get out of there without any trouble. If they know you're going to turn them in, they will try to stop you.

You walk out of the workshop and then rush down the long, gold-encrusted hallways until you reach the Emperor's office. You go inside.

"Sir, I have terrible news," you say. "The suit is not real. The tailors are really former senators. They are trying to betray you."

Turn the page.

You tell the Emperor about Scarlett and Luisa's plot to have him wear a pretend spacesuit during the parade. He wouldn't be able to breathe in the moon's atmosphere. Worst-case scenario, he would explode under the pressure.

"I'm sorry, sir," you say. "I know how excited you were about the spacesuit."

The Emperor bangs his fist on the desk. "I knew it!" he yells. "That is why I got rid of those senators in the first place. You can't trust them!"

He orders his secret police to arrest the senators. The senators don't go quietly. The two women fire their laser-powered guns at the cops. More secret police run into the senators' room. Soon the women are overpowered.

The former senators are sent away. Nobody knows where they went. The Emperor does not share those kinds of secrets.

After that, life goes back to how it was. The Emperor passes more damaging laws. Soon people are not allowed to go to the hospital unless they give the Emperor a million *Lunas,* or moon dollars. Everyone must pay steep taxes directly to the Emperor. His mansion is decorated with more and more gold, rubies, and diamonds.

In short, life on the moon is terrible for everyone but the Emperor. Suffering is all around you. You are always worried about making a mistake and disappearing like the senators.

THE END
To follow another path, turn to page 9.

"I'm in. The Emperor needs to be stopped," you say. "This is a brilliant idea. He is so vain, he will believe there is an amazing spacesuit here. All we have to do is tell him how great he looks."

"We have to get him to wear the suit in the spacewalk parade," Scarlett says. "He will instantly die without a real spacesuit on."

"We can restore democracy," Luisa adds.

"We'll be heroes," you say.

The two former senators arrive in the Emperor's grand bedroom to deliver the spacesuit. You stand by the Emperor and exclaim how amazing it looks.

"Look at that. It's a marvel of modern science!" you say.

The Emperor stares into the box. "Are you sure you like it?" he says, raising an eyebrow.

"Oh, yes," you say to the Emperor. "I have never seen anything quite like this spacesuit."

"Try it on," Luisa says. She lifts the imaginary suit out of the box and holds out her hands low, as if the Emperor could step into the pants.

"Hold on a minute," the Emperor says. He grabs you by the collar. "What is going on here?"

This is not good. You need to convince him that everything is okay. He needs to believe that the suit is real and nobody means to betray him. Or you could turn in the senators and try to save your own skin.

To try to convince the Emperor to go to the parade, go to page 57.

To turn in the senators, turn to page 61.

The only hope for a fair government and a safe world is to get rid of the Emperor. Even if you are killed or thrown in prison, you have to try.

"I don't blame you for being skeptical, sir," you say. "The suit is so beautiful, it is hard to believe that someone could make such a thing. But I have tracked the progress of these tailors. Their craftsmanship is beyond compare. This spacesuit is the best in the galaxy."

"But it looks . . ." the Emperor begins. You start to sweat. Will he trust his own eyes? Or will his vanity get the better of him?

"It looks . . . so out of this world," he finishes.

"It sure does," you agree. "Why don't you put it on? I can't wait for everyone in the moon nation to see you wearing this unbelievable suit."

That seems to do the trick. The Emperor puts on the suit and goes to the loading bay to prepare for the parade. You and the tailors watch from the safety of the viewing platform built into the royal mansion.

The parade begins. It's huge. There are soldiers, musicians, dancers, acrobats, clowns, large animals, more soldiers, and more music. Everyone rides in large, flat ships with clear bubbles over the top. The bubble tops allow the crowd to see them while protecting the people inside from the moon's atmosphere.

The Emperor's ship comes last. He likes to ride in a flat ship without a bubble top to show how tough he is. He is always protected by a spacesuit. But this parade is different. Everyone can see that he is in his underwear.

As soon as the ship moves out from the loading bay, the Emperor expands like a balloon. His secret police try to help. But there is nothing they can do. Within seconds, he suffocates. The Emperor's reign has come to an end.

"That was horrifying," you say as the space ambulance takes him away.

"That was the price of democracy," Scarlett says solemnly.

She is right about that. You and the senators re-establish the senate and the rule of law. You run for president and win. You work hard to create a moon nation where everyone feels welcome and safe.

THE END
To follow another path, turn to page 9.

"There's something I have to tell you," you say to the Emperor. "These two tailors are really former senators. They are plotting against you. There is no spacesuit."

Luisa and Scarlett are taken aback. They trusted you. "If you can't see the suit, then *you* are disloyal to the Emperor," Luisa says. "You are a traitor!"

"I am not the traitor here, and you know it," you say.

"Stop this fighting," the Emperor demands. He pushes a button on his watch and several armed guards come into the room. "I don't think there is one spacesuit here," he says, looking in the box. "I think there are *three* suits. And let me see here . . . one, two, three," he counts, pointing to you, Luisa, and Scarlett. "Well that is convenient, isn't it? Put them on."

"What?" you say. "There's nothing here."

"I said put them on," he barks.

"Sir, I was on your side," you say. "I tried to save you."

"Only after you knew your plan wouldn't work," he says. "Now it is too late."

The guards point their guns at you. You, Scarlett, and Luisa pretend to put on the fake spacesuits. Then the secret police secure you to a spaceship. The ship is flat, without a protective, air-filled bubble top. The parade starts.

You, Luisa, and Scarlett are in the last ship. You watch the musicians and entertainers pass by. People are cheering. Music plays. It is only a matter of time until your ship moves. Then you will be crushed by the moon's atmosphere.

THE END
To follow another path, turn to page 9.

You and Boris agree to keep the secret. Deep down, you both know the Emperor needs to be stopped. The moon nation is in chaos. You hope that if you say nothing, the Emperor will wear the suit outside for the parade. Unprotected from the atmosphere, he will die. Then the moon has a chance of being a fair, safe place to live.

Days later, Scarlett and Luisa show up with a metal box. They open it up and show the suit inside to the emperor. You and Boris exclaim how great the suit is. You wink at Scarlett so she knows you are on her side. With all the compliments, it is easy to convince the Emperor that the invisible spacesuit is real. All you have to do is keep reminding him how great he looks.

63

Just as planned, the Emperor wears his new spacesuit to the parade outside. He quickly dies.

Turn the page.

That night, you and Boris celebrate with Luisa and Scarlett.

"We did it," you say. "Your plan worked."

"Now, for the best part of the plan," Scarlett says. As you watch, her hands turn into tentacles. Her face morphs into a bug-eyed hairless blob. Luisa does the same.

"What is going on?" Boris asks. He looks terrified. You are terrified too. You have never seen space aliens like this before.

"Now that we are rid of the Emperor, the moon is ours to rule!" Scarlett says.

You and Boris run out of the room as fast as you can. You alert the secret police and the military on the moon. They prepare for an invasion. When the aliens come, they attack. For years after, life is war. Just like under the Emperor, you never know who you can trust. Fire and death fill the moon base. Great ships with scary-looking laser cannons float outside the windows. You don't expect to live long in these conditions. Maybe the Emperor wasn't so bad after all.

THE END
To follow another path, turn to page 9.

"We have to tell the Emperor," you say. "If we don't and he finds out, he will make us disappear."

"True," Boris agrees. "Even if he dies out in the parade, the secret police will figure out we were part of it. Then *they* will make us disappear."

"We just have to make sure he does not go to the parade thinking that he's wearing a spacesuit," you say.

You request a meeting with the Emperor and tell him everything. "Scarlett and Luisa are really senators. They are plotting to kill you," you say.

"That's ridiculous," the Emperor says. He laughs. "I knew you were jealous of my power and good looks, but this is really embarrassing."

"Sir," Boris says. "It's true. You must not put on that suit!"

"Bah!" The Emperor throws you out.

The senators deliver the imaginary spacesuit. Just as you expected, the Emperor says that he loves it. The two senators flatter him. They tell him that he is the most powerful man in the universe. He deserves the best spacesuit.

As the parade draws near, the Emperor goes into his inner chamber and puts on his suit. When he comes back out, you plead with him.

"Sir," you say, "there is clearly no suit! Please do not go out to theparade in space. You will die without a real suit to protect you."

"Maybe you're not just jealous," the Emperor says. "Maybe you really are a traitor. Are you?"

"Of course not, sir," you say.

Turn the page.

As the Emperor gets into position for the parade, Boris has an idea. "I've been working on a super-secret project that might help us," he says. "It's a bubble projector. If you shoot it into space, it will capture things in a safe atmosphere."

"Let's try it," you say.

"It's still being tested," he says. "But we don't have much choice." He goes into the basement and returns with a cannonlike machine.

You and Boris get into a small ship and position yourselves over the parade. Ships float by playing music. Soon the cargo bay opens up and the Emperor's ship begins to move out. Boris aims the cannon at him and pulls the trigger.

BLOORG! A bluish-white cone shoots out of the cannon. It turns invisible as it travels toward the Emperor.

You follow it on a computer screen as it turns into a bubble and surrounds him. The Emperor moves along the parade route, smiling and waving. He is so happy. Everyone cheers and cries out their support. They are amazed that a human can travel in the moon's atmosphere without a spacesuit on. He must be even more powerful than they thought!

Afterward, everyone thinks the Emperor has magical powers. They obey everything he commands. Scarlett and Luisa run away, never to be seen again.

But you are punished too. The Emperor decides that you and Boris are traitors because you did not believe in the suit. He has his guards slam you into a thin, tin-can spaceship. As you hurtle out into space, you notice that the ship is breaking apart already.

You will end up somewhere in the deepest, darkest part of space. Eventually your ship will disintegrate. Temperatures will be impossibly low. Your body will expand to twice its size and freeze solid. You sure could use a magical spacesuit right about now.

THE END
To follow another path, turn to page 9.

CHAPTER 4

A FRIGHTENINGLY FANCY FEAST

Emily P. Roor is a wealthy trendsetter with a large following online. She is beautiful and loves taking selfies. She is always in style, and everyone wants to be seen with her.

Emily is also a jerk. She is shallow and self-centered. Even her friends think so. She is obsessed with fame and being admired. Emily spends lots of money on lavish banquets. She only invites the most famous people to join her for amazing food. People post selfies on social media with the hashtag #dinnerwiththeEmPRoor.

Of course, most people can't score an invite. Emily loves to exclude people from her fancy parties. She laughs knowing they feel bad.

You are part of Emily's inner circle of friends. She's nice to you, but you're sick of the way she treats everyone else.

One day two of your mutual friends, Lupe and Henry, convince Emily to throw another party. You're kind of surprised. Emily made fun of them online pretty badly last week. Maybe they are trying to get back on her good side. Henry recommends a famous chef he knows.

"This chef is so famous, *everyone* will want to be seen at this party," says Henry.

"The social media presence will be off the charts," adds Lupe. "It will be the fanciest, most lavish party of all time."

The day of the party, Emily is barking orders at the people decorating the dance hall. She sees you come in the door.

"Let's go meet the chef," Emily says, grabbing your hand and leading you into the kitchen.

"Chef Katia, how is the food coming along?" Emily asks. "I expect perfection."

"This food is going to be *very* fancy," Chef Katia assures you both. "Very highbrow."

"I certainly hope so," Emily says.

"It's so fancy that people who are *not* fancy will not like it," Chef Katia continues. "If someone says the food tastes bad, you will know that person is beneath you and undeserving of your time."

"Make sure to post their loser faces all over social media," the chef's assistant adds.

This idea delights Emily. She loves finding fame at other people's expense. Emily leaves the kitchen with an extra spring in her step. You stay behind to see what the chef is making.

"It looks great," you tell her.

"Of course it does. Would you like a taste?" Chef Katia asks. There are nice-looking puff pastries sitting on the table. "These are stuffed with caviar—and a *very special* ingredient."

You thank her and try the pastry. But the second it hits your tongue, you want to throw up. It is horrible! In fact, it tastes like old dog food. You desperately want to spit it out. But if Emily hears you don't like the food, you know she will make your life miserable.

To spit out the pastry, turn to page 78.

To pretend you love it, turn to page 80.

You are not going to swallow this nasty stuff. There must be something wrong with it.

"Chef, this is disgusting!" you say, spitting it out into a napkin.

Chef Katia smiles. "Is it, now?"

"You can't serve this. I mean, is this spoiled?" you ask.

"It's not spoiled," she replies. "It is just very fancy food. I am surprised you don't like it. I thought you were one of Emily's wealthy friends. I guess I was wrong. Shall I let Emily know you don't like my food?"

You don't want Emily to find out you hate the food. She will destroy you on social media.

"No, no. That's not necessary," you say. "I was just . . . testing you. Of course it's delicious. Keep up the good work."

"Be sure to tell Emily how good it is," Katia's assistant says.

"Of course," you say. "Thank you."

But as you step out of the kitchen, you see a can of dog food on the shelf. What is that doing in the kitchen? Emily doesn't have a dog.

"Enjoy the party," Chef Katia says, smirking.

To spy on **Chef Katia,** turn to page 83.

To just get out of there, turn to page 87.

"Mmm!" you lie. "Delicious." You nod with approval, hoping you look convincing. But you feel your stomach twist and turn. You hope you can keep it down.

"Thank you," Chef Katia says. "It's an old family recipe. Would you like another one?"

"No!" you yell. "I mean, thank you but no. I, uh, I want to save room for dinner." You back away.

"Well," Chef Katia says, "please let Emily know how much you like the food. I am a little nervous cooking for someone so famous. I hope she likes it!" She gives you a big fake smile.

She doesn't look nervous, you think. *She looks like she's up to something.*

"I will let her know," you say.

You leave the kitchen and head right to the bathroom. You rinse out your mouth. Then you catch your breath.

Eventually, you head back out. The party has already started. Guests are arriving. People are talking, laughing, and enjoying cold drinks. Some are dancing.

You see Emily right away. She is laughing with a group of people. One of them is a famous movie star. Emily sees you.

"Come over here!" Emily calls to you. "I want you to meet Chris."

You would love to meet the movie star. Chris Phatt is in your favorite movie. You walk over and shake hands with everyone. You tell a funny story, and Chris laughs. Things are going great.

Turn the page.

That's when Chef Katia comes out of the kitchen and announces that dinner is served.

Emily turns to you. "I know you stayed in the kitchen and tried the pastries. What did you think?"

You hesitate. If you say the food was disgusting, Emily will make fun of you in front of everyone. What will Chris Phatt think? You will never go to another fancy party again. But if you say you liked it, you will have to sit for dinner and eat it in front of everyone.

To tell Emily the truth, turn to page 91.

To tell her the food was delicious, turn to page 94.

On your way out of the kitchen, you grab a paperclip off the desk. Then you walk out into the ballroom. The party has started and it's getting crowded. A band is playing. A few people are dancing. Some people are laughing over in the corner as they look at their phones. Emily probably made fun of someone again.

You sneak along the edge of the ballroom floor and into the hallway. At the end of the hall, there is a door that leads to the back of the kitchen. It is locked. You pull out the paperclip and unbend it.

Let's hope this works, you think.

You carefully slip the paperclip into the lock, move it just so, and . . . *CLICK!* The door opens.

You slip silently inside and shut the door behind you. Then you look around. You are in the back of the kitchen by the pantry and the loading area. Full trash cans line the wall. Out front, you hear Chef Katia and her assistant chatting quietly. You know you'll have to be quick and sneaky.

You kneel down and check the labels on the food in the trash. You are shocked at what you see. There are empty cans of dog food. There's also an old vacuum cleaner bag full of lint and dust. On your left, you find a baggie full of toenail clippings. There's even a carton of earthworms from a bait store.

"Ew!" you say out loud. Then you slap your hands over your mouth.

"Hello?" Chef Katia calls.

You crawl into the pantry and hold your breath. You can hear Chef Katia peeking around, but then people come into the front part of the kitchen. It's Lupe and Henry. You hold still and listen.

"How's it going?" Henry asks.

"Oh, it's going really well," Katia says. "Everything is all set."

"Oh boy!" Lupe says. "I cannot wait."

What is Chef Katia up to? Do Lupe and Henry know the food is bad? Should you say something to them?

86

To sneak away, go to page 87.
To tell Lupe and Henry about the chef, turn to page 97.

The first thing you need to do is wash the awful taste out of your mouth. You go the bathroom and drink a bunch of water. Your stomach rumbles unhappily. You try to ignore it. You hide out in the bathroom for a while as people arrive for the party. You'd rather not talk to Emily alone if you can help it.

When you come out, the party is in full swing. You see a famous author talking to a baseball player. The owner of a soccer team is getting some punch. And there's Chris Phatt! He's one of your favorite actors. It always surprises you how popular Emily is.

At the table, everyone is chatting about the food. They can't wait. The waiters bring out plates, and everyone starts eating. Everyone except you.

The author sniffs her pastry and politely puts it down. "No thank you," she says.

After a while, the guests start to fidget uncomfortably. That's when it happens.

Chris Phatt leans his head under the table and pukes on the floor. The owner of the soccer team holds his hand over his mouth and tries to run. Vomit sprays between his fingers like a sprinkler. You and the author just stare at each other.

Even Emily runs to the bathroom. When she returns, everyone is on their phones posting selfies and pictures of puke pools. The #dinnerwiththeEmPRoor hashtag is full of awful images and terrible posts about Emily.

Emily quickly pulls out her phone to do damage control.

"The food was amazing," she types. "Everyone threw up so they had enough room in their stomachs for more!"

Then Emily posts a selfie with Chris Phatt from earlier in the night. She writes, "Another fabulous dinner! #dontbejealous #dinnerwiththeEmPRoor."

Emily has so many loyal fans that everyone who wasn't at the party believes her. Her story is ridiculous, but it doesn't matter. Even people who were at the party begin to question their own memories. Soon they are posting about how great the party was. Somehow, Emily becomes even more famous than before.

THE END
To follow another path, turn to page 9.

You are one of Emily's oldest friends. Surely she would believe you. And yes, Emily can be awful. But you don't want to destroy her reputation either. You decide to be honest.

"Emily," you say, "there's something wrong with the food. It doesn't taste right."

"Oh, dear," Emily says, a vicious smile creeping at her lips. "How would *you* know what tastes right?" She laughs. People at the party look over.

Chris doesn't laugh though. He says, "What do you mean it doesn't taste right?"

Emily and her friends are laughing at you and whispering. "Doesn't taste right? Ha!"

91

"It just tasted off," you say to the group. "But maybe it was just the piece I tried. I'm sure it's fine." But you know better.

Turn the page.

At dinner, you watch in horror as everyone eats the food. Any minute now, everyone is going to get sick all over this table. It's too bad Emily didn't listen to you.

But nothing happens. You look at Emily. She takes a dainty bite of what looks like vacuum bag dust and swallows. She doesn't even flinch! You can't believe it. What's worse, nobody admits the food is terrible. They continue to eat. They take selfies with Emily and post them online. Emily continues to make fun of you. It's a miserable night.

You start to think that the food really *could* be too upscale for you. But then you notice the chef. She and her assistant are over by the door with Henry and Lupe. They are recording everyone and laughing. What's so funny? Then it hits you. They did all of this on purpose.

Henry and Lupe are trying to get back at Emily by embarrassing her and her vain friends. It's going to be all over the internet soon.

But the next day, all you see are Emily's posts about how simple and drab you are. It spreads like wildfire across the internet. You lose all your online fans—even your little sister won't follow you. Every time you go out, people look at you funny like they recognize you. Some even laugh.

Henry and Lupe will have to try harder next time if they want to take Emily down. You hope they do. But you won't be around to see it. This was probably your last dinner party.

THE END
To follow another path, turn to page 9.

"Oh, my goodness," you say. "It was so good, I didn't even want to finish eating it. *So good.*"

Chris says, "I've really been looking forward to this. Thanks for inviting me, Emily."

"Thank you for coming," she says, but you can tell that she thinks she's doing him a favor.

You sit down to dinner and force yourself to eat. You have another dog food pastry. It's just as bad as the first time you tried it. You have a serving of everything else. It's all terrible. In between bites, you clench your jaw shut so nothing comes shooting back out. You flex your stomach muscles to keep everything down. All around you, people are enjoying dinner. Sweat pours down your temples. By the end, your stomach muscles hurt from holding the food down. Your head swirls.

You can't hold back any longer. You bend over as if you are tying your shoe. But really you barf onto the floor under the table. When you sit up, nobody has noticed. You feel relief for a second. But then the room spins. You fall backward onto the floor. Just before you pass out, you look up. Emily is standing over you.

"Drama queen," Emily says, crossing her arms.

A friend takes you home. You lie on the couch. You feel miserable the whole night. Emily never even texts you to see how you are.

Some friend, you think.

The next day, you still feel terrible. But your head has stopped spinning, so you turn on the TV. There's a parade on. And who is riding in the next float? Emily P. Roor.

Turn the page.

You roll your eyes. But as you are about to change the channel, you hear the announcer.

"Famous internet fashion icon, Emily P. Roor is here, folks," the announcer says. "And . . . Oh, dear. She's throwing up all over the float!"

The camera zooms in. Emily finishes puking and wipes her mouth. Then she stands tall again. Emily smiles and keeps waving at the crowd. There's a big vomit stain on her blouse.

All her fans watching that parade think it's a new trend. Fashion designers start making vomit-stained shirts. Stores sell out in minutes. Emily has started the next big thing. And she's more popular than ever.

THE END
To follow another path, turn to page 9.

After Henry and Lupe leave the kitchen, you sneak out the way you came in. Back in the ballroom, you scan the party until you find the pair. They're laughing.

"Lupe! Henry!" you say. "Something weird is going on. I know this is going to sound crazy. But I think the chef is feeding people, like, garbage and stuff."

Lupe and Henry look at each other and laugh.

You say, "I'm serious! I saw vacuum bag of dust and a bunch of toenail clippings in the kitchen. Even worms! I think I ate a pastry made of dog food."

"Oh, sorry about that," Lupe says. "We didn't mean for you to get caught up in this."

"What are you talking about?" you ask.

Turn the page.

Henry rubs his hands together and grins. "Remember when Emily roasted us on social media last week? I lost half of my followers! It's payback time."

"We are going to make her and all these phony fakers eat all that garbage," says Lupe. "That's what this whole party is about. Nobody will have the courage to complain—they're too afraid of Emily's power. We get to watch how far they will go to get her approval."

"What if Emily complains?" you ask. "I mean, what if *she* says the food is bad?"

"That would be the best part," Henry says. "Then we can all say *she* is not fancy enough."

At dinner, you sit next to Henry and Lupe. Emily is across the table. The food is served, and everyone starts eating.

There is a moment when things can go either way. You see that Emily is thinking. The food is obviously terrible. Maybe she'll say so.

Henry leans over to whisper to you. "We need to convince Emily to eat! Come on, you know she deserves it."

Henry is right. Emily has not only been mean to Henry and Lupe. She's been mean to many others, including you. But is this going too far?

To eat some of your own food and show Emily it's okay, turn to page 100.

To tell her you don't like the food, turn to page 103.

You decide to encourage Emily by eating some of the food yourself. You hold your breath and have a forkful of toenail supreme. You chew and chew, but those toenails are hard to break down. Emily watches you.

"What are you doing? This stuff is disgusting!" she says finally. "I can't believe you ate it!" She looks around the room. "You must really be desperate to fit in," Emily says.

You think fast. You decide to laugh. "Oh, Emily, you know I don't care about fitting in. I just love fine food."

"This is *not* fine food," she says. But she doesn't look so sure. Some of the guests are looking to you for the answer. So you take another bite.

"Mmm," you say. "It's good. And really fancy!"

The other guests follow your lead and start eating. Someone snaps a selfie with you. Then someone else does the same. They go up on social media. Over the next few days, Emily loses most of her followers. They all flock to you! Everyone watches you for the next trends. They start hashtags about you. Emily P. Roor is so *yesterday*. Now you are the reigning internet celebrity.

THE END
To follow another path, turn to page 9.

"This food is terrible," you say. You raise your voice so not only Emily will hear, but anyone else nearby. "This food is awful. I'd never eat this."

Emily gets a big smile on her face. "I knew it!" she says. "You are so simple. So drab! You are not even the tiniest bit fancy!"

Emily takes a huge bite out of a dog food pastry. She gobbles down several forkfuls of earthworms. She absolutely inhales the baked vacuum cleaner dust. She eats it all, smiling the whole way. She doesn't notice that everyone else at the table has stopped. They know the food is gross. They watch in horror as the fancy socialite Emily P. Roor devours the worst food they have ever tasted. Some whip out their phones and take videos. When Emily is finished, she stands up from the table and faces you.

"And that is why you will always be beneath me," Emily gloats. "That is why . . ."

But before Emily can finish, she throws up. A lot. She pukes on the table. She spews on her lap. She vomits on her shoes. She upchucks on a movie star. She ralphs in the punch bowl.

All of Emily's so-called friends laugh. They posted photos online with the hashtag #dinnerdisasterwiththeEmPRoor.

Emily is absolutely roasted online. She is humiliated. You actually feel a bit sorry for her. When she throws another fancy dinner party, you show up. But nobody else does.

Meanwhile, Chef Katia is more popular than ever. She posts photos of food with the hashtag #whatwouldEmPRooreat. Everyone tries to guess if it has garbage in it or not. Dishes are rated on a scale of 1 to 5 Emily vomit faces.

One day Henry and Lupe come to your home. "We need a plan," Henry says. "We have to get rid of Chef Katia."

"I have an idea," you say. "Does she need any new clothes?"

THE END
To follow another path, turn to page 9.

THE EMPEROR'S NEW CLOTHES THROUGH HISTORY

When Hans Christian Andersen was a child, he stood in a crowd with his mother. He wanted to catch a glimpse of Frederick VI, the King of Denmark. When the king came into view, Hans was surprised. He thought the king would be something grand and unique.

"Oh, he's nothing more than a human being!" Hans cried.

Years later, Hans Christian Andersen wrote "The Emperor's New Clothes." By then he was an established author. The story was included in the third volume of his collection *Fairy Tales Told for Children*, published in 1837.

The inspiration for the tale came from a much older source—*Of that which happened to a King and Three Impostors*. This Spanish tale was written in 1338.

Andersen changed the story so it was about vanity. The Emperor's clothes would be invisible to anyone who was not worthy of their position or social class. At first he left the ending as it had been in the original story. The Emperor's subjects simply admired his clothes.

The book was already at the printer when Andersen had an idea for a new ending. Perhaps he remembered that day when he saw the King of Denmark for the first time. Andersen added the child who cried out, "The Emperor has no clothes!"

The story has been retold in many ways over the years, including on TV and in movies. A recent example is the 2018 HBO Family animated feature, *The Emperor's Newest Clothes*.

"The Emperor's New Clothes" is one of Hans Christian Andersen's most famous stories. To this day, the phrase "the Emperor has no clothes" is a way to describe someone who acts like something is true when they know it is not.

OTHER PATHS TO EXPLORE

1. In chapter 2, the sheriff must decide to either tell the mayor about the crooked tailors or go along with the plan. What would you do if you were the sheriff?

2. In chapter 4, the fairy tale takes place in modern times. How is the story different from the original fairy tale? How is it the same?

3. In the classic version of "The Emperor's New Clothes," the Emperor is tricked into wearing his underwear in front of his subjects. What do you think the lesson is for the Emperor? How would you feel if you were the Emperor?